Car Goes Far

I Like to Read® Books
You will like all of them!

Paperback and Hardcover

Boy, Bird, and Dog by David McPhail

Dinosaurs Don't, Dinosaurs Do by Steve Björkman

The Lion and the Mice
by Rebecca Emberley and Ed Emberley

See Me Run by Paul Meisel
A Theodor Seuss Geisel Award Honor Book

Hardcover

Car Goes Far by Michael Garland

Fish Had a Wish by Michael Garland

The Fly Flew In by David Catrow

I Have a Garden by Bob Barner

I Will Try by Marilyn Janovitz

Late Nate in a Race by Emily Arnold McCully

Look! by Ted Lewin

Mice on Ice
by Rebecca Emberley and Ed Emberley

Pig Has a Plan by Ethan Long

Sam and the Big Kids by Emily Arnold McCully

See Me Dig by Paul Meisel

Sick Day by David McPhail

You Can Do It! by Betsy Lewin

Visit holidayhouse.com to read more
about I Like to Read® Books.

Car Goes Far

by Michael Garland

Holiday House / New York

To my son Kevin

I LIKE TO READ is a registered trademark of Holiday House, Inc.

Copyright © 2013 by Michael Garland
All Rights Reserved
HOLIDAY HOUSE is registered in the U.S. Patent and Trademark Office.
Printed and Bound March 2017 at Tien Wah Press, Johor Bahru, Johor, Malaysia.
The artwork was created with mixed digital tools.
www.holidayhouse.com
5 7 9 10 8 6 4

Library of Congress Cataloging-in-Publication Data
Garland, Michael, 1952-
Car goes far / by Michael Garland. — 1st ed.
p. cm. — (I like to read)
Summary: After an adventure, a shiny, clean car is in desperate need of a wash.
ISBN 978-0-8234-2598-3 (hardcover)
[1. Automobiles—Fiction. 2. Car washes—Fiction.] I. Title.
PZ7.G18413Car 2013
[E]—dc23
2011049242

ISBN 978-0-8234-3058-1 (paperback)
GRL D

Car looks good.

Car goes.

Car goes far.

Oh, no! Mud gets on Car.

Oh, no! Smoke gets on Car.

Oh, no!
Birds make a mess on Car.

Car does not look good now.
Car is sad.

Car must wash.

Car gets wet.
Splash, splash.

Car gets suds.

Car gets a rub.
Mmmmmmm.

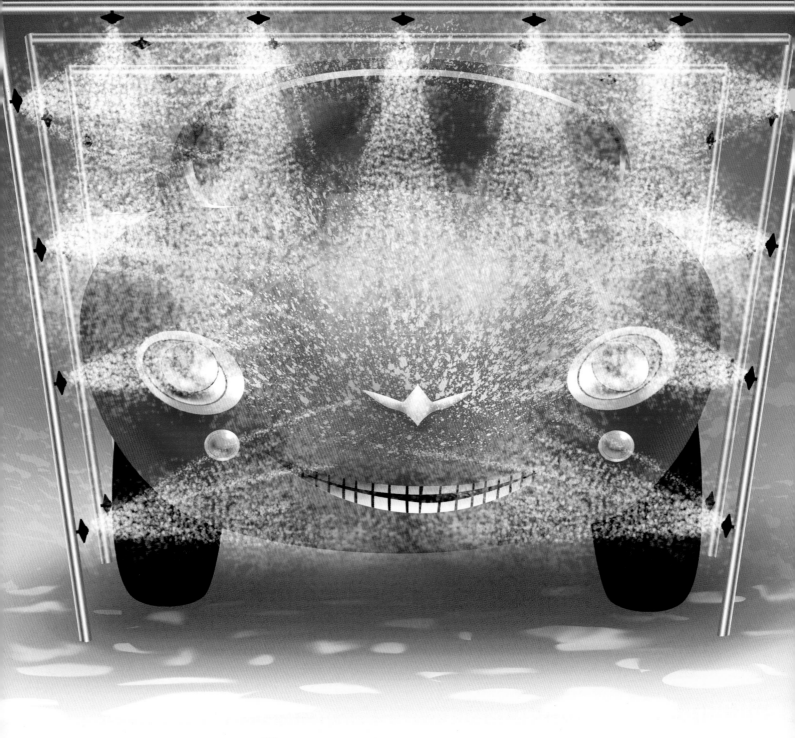

Car gets wet again.

Car gets dry.

Car looks good again!

I Like to Read® Books in Paperback
You will like all of them!

Boy, Bird, and Dog by David McPhail

Car Goes Far by Michael Garland

Dinosaurs Don't, Dinosaurs Do
by Steve Björkman

Fish Had a Wish by Michael Garland

The Fly Flew In by David Catrow

I Have a Garden by Bob Barner

I Will Try by Marilyn Janovitz

Late Nate in a Race
by Emily Arnold McCully

The Lion and the Mice
by Rebecca Emberley and Ed Emberley

Look! by Ted Lewin

Mice on Ice
by Rebecca Emberley and Ed Emberley

Pig Has a Plan by Ethan Long

Sam and the Big Kids by Emily Arnold McCully

See Me Dig by Paul Meisel

See Me Run by Paul Meisel
A Theodor Seuss Geisel Award Honor Book

Sick Day by David McPhail

You Can Do It! by Betsy Lewin

Visit http://www.holidayhouse.com/I-Like-to-Read/
for more about I Like to Read® books, including
flash cards, reproducibles, and the complete list of titles.